W9-BLD-465

RANGER in TIME

Escape from the Great Earthquake

KATE MESSNER

illustrated by
KELLEY McMORRIS

Scholastic Press / New York

Library of Congress Cataloging-in-Publication Data
Names: Messner, Kate, author. | McMorris, Kelley, illustrator. | Messner, Kate. Ranger in time.
Title: Escape from the great earthquake / Kate Messner ; illustrated by Kelley McMorris.
Description: New York : Scholastic Inc., 2017. | Series: Ranger in time ; 6 | Summary: This time Ranger, the time-traveling golden retriever, finds himself in San Francisco in the middle of the great 1906 earthquake, and his mission is obviously to get a young Chinese immigrant, Lily Chen, to safety, but as they make their way through the ruined and burning city Ranger finds that he must also accomplish something else—finding Lily, who was sold as a servant by her parents, a new family who will care for her.
Identifiers: LCCN 2016043023
Subjects: LCSH: Golden retriever—Juvenile fiction. | Time travel—Juvenile fiction. | San Francisco Earthquake and Fire, Calif., 1906—Juvenile fiction. | Earthquakes—California—San Francisco—Juvenile fiction. | Chinese—California—San Francisco—History—Juvenile fiction. | Adventure stories. | San Francisco (Calif.)—History—Juvenile fiction. | CYAC: Golden retriever—Fiction. | Dogs—Fiction. | Time travel—Fiction. | San Francisco Earthquake and Fire, Calif., 1906—Fiction. | Chinese Americans—Fiction. | Adventure and adventurers—Fiction. | San Francisco (Calif.)—History—20th century—Fiction. | GSAFD: Adventure fiction. | LCGFT: Action and adventure fiction.
Classification: LCC PZ7.M5615 Es 2017 | DDC 813.6 [Fic]—dc23
LC record available at https://lccn.loc.gov/2016043023

ISBN 978-0-545-90984-6

10 9 8 7 6 5 4 3 2 1   17 18 19 20 21

Printed in the United States of America   113
First printing 2017

Book design by Ellen Duda

For Kelley, illustrator extraordinaire

Chapter 1

MORNING OF THE EARTH DRAGON

At first, Lily Chen thought it was another nightmare. The roaring sea. The slamming waves. So often, her dreams took her back to the crowded, lurching ship that had brought her across the ocean to San Francisco five years ago.

But this nightmare didn't end when Lily opened her eyes.

An angry roar shook the mission home where she lived with fifty other girls and women. Lily sat up in bed as the mirror over the dresser crashed to the floor. It smashed into shining pieces that danced and skidded over the wood. The whole house rocked as if an angry giant shook it in his palm. The window rattled itself free and crashed to the street below.

Lily's bed jumped up and down and sideways until she was thrown to the floor. She crawled to the open window and pulled herself up to look outside. The street was a rolling wave of cobblestones.

People stood in their nightshirts, looking up to the sky. An old man raced into the street in his bare feet, shouting, "Aiyaaa, dei lung zan! Aiyaaa, dei lung zan!" which means "The earth dragon is wiggling!"

Lily understood this was one of California's earthquakes. Usually, they were trembles that shook pictures from the walls. But today, Lily felt like one of the rats that the neighborhood dogs liked to catch and thrash about. She staggered back to her bed and clung to the headboard.

The house swayed like a ferryboat in a storm. Ceiling timbers groaned. Chimney bricks crashed onto the roof. Lily's room filled with dust as the plaster walls cracked and crumbled.

It felt as if the shaking might never end, but finally the house settled. Lily picked her way through the broken mirror pieces to the door.

It was jammed shut, stuck in the twisted door frame. But Lily was big for her age, and strong. As a servant in Chinatown, she'd lugged around pails of stew and baskets of vegetables every day. She yanked until the frame let go and sent her flying backward across the glass-strewn floor.

"Are you all right?" a voice called from the hallway. It was Donaldina Cameron, the woman who ran the mission house. The girls called her Lo Mo, or "old mother," but she was nothing like the mother Lily remembered from home. Lily's real mother smelled of earth from working the farm. Her real mother was far away over the ocean, in China's Guangdong province.

Lo Mo's mission house was better than being beaten as a servant, but it was a long way from home.

"We've been shaken, but this good house is still standing," Lo Mo told the girls. "Come downstairs, and we'll see about breakfast."

Lily and the other girls climbed over fallen bookshelves and got themselves dressed. The quake had rattled pictures from the walls and toppled dressers, but somehow the fishbowl on the little hallway table had survived.

"Gum Gum!" Lily rushed over, knelt down, and smiled at the little fish. Some of his water had sloshed out onto the table, but he was all

right. "Your golden color certainly brought you good fortune this morning," she said.

When Lily went downstairs, her heart sank. The girls had cleaned the house spotless that week. They'd swept and dusted and draped a beautiful fishnet in the chapel room to get ready for the annual meeting of the people who ran the home. Now all the dishes had been tossed about and broken. The chimney had collapsed. How would they even cook?

Lo Mo settled everyone down, and soon there was breakfast. Someone brought baskets of bread from a bakery nearby. Another neighbor appeared with apples and a kettle of tea. Lily sat with the others at the little white tables and recited a Psalm from the Bible.

"The Lord is my Shepherd; I shall not want . . ."

Lily's mind wandered. Even as the girls ate, there was talk of packing and going to the

Presbyterian church on Van Ness Avenue until it was certain the home would be safe.

Lo Mo told them to gather just a few things. They finished eating and set to packing up bundles of bedding, clothes, and a little food.

Outside, Chinatown buzzed with noise. Doors slammed. Voices filled with worry, and fear drifted through the broken windows. When Lily returned to the kitchen and looked out the door, she understood why.

The sky was full of dust clouds where buildings had collapsed. In the distance, half a dozen dark plumes of smoke rose into the quiet sky.

The earthquake was only the beginning.

Chapter 2

SORTING AND SHARING

"These don't fit me anymore," Sadie said, holding up a pair of jeans.

"They're still in good shape," her mother said. "Fold them and add them to the pile."

Luke and Sadie had been sorting clothes all morning. Their church was collecting donations for some refugee families that would arrive soon.

Ranger wished Luke and Sadie would finish and take him outside to play. He plopped down on a pile of Luke's old sweatshirts to wait.

"I'm not sure Ranger understands what's going on," Luke said, laughing.

"I'm not sure I understand, either," Sadie said as she added another shirt to her pile. "Why are the families coming here if their homes are so far away? And why can't they bring their own clothes?"

"Because they had to leave very quickly," Mom said. "Refugees are people who are forced to leave their homes because of war or disaster or some other reason. There's often little time to plan or pack."

"That's why they need our help, right?" Luke shook out a pair of snow pants. "To get settled in a new home where it's safe."

"Right," Dad said. "These boxes are pretty full. Let's load up the car."

Ranger followed Luke and Sadie outside. While they put boxes in the trunk, Ranger sniffed around the yard. It had rained the night before, so the grass smelled of earth-worms and mud. And . . . *squirrel!*

Ranger perked up his ears and looked around.

There! It was under the picnic table, twitch-ing its fluffy tail.

Ranger bounded toward the squirrel, and it took off running. He chased it around the yard, past the bird feeder, and through the garden. Then the squirrel ran up a tree. It looked down at Ranger from a branch and twitched its tail again.

Ranger barked at the squirrel like he always did after one got away. He loved chasing squir-rels. That was the reason he wasn't an official search-and-rescue dog.

Ranger had been through weeks of search-and-rescue training with Luke and Dad. He'd learned to track people by following scent trails in the air and on the ground. He'd practiced finding Luke lots of times. It didn't matter if Luke was hiding in thick woods or in a barrel or in a tunnel under the snow. Ranger found him every time.

But search-and-rescue dogs weren't allowed to chase squirrels while they were working. Even if the work was only practice or a test. Ranger would never run off to chase a squirrel if a person really needed his help. But on the day Ranger took his test, he knew Luke was just pretending. A squirrel had raced past, and Ranger couldn't resist its fluffy, twitchy tail.

"You coming back in, Ranger?" Luke called. "We need to pack up some more boxes."

Ranger went inside. As he passed through the mudroom, he heard a sound coming from his dog bed.

Ranger knew what it was. The old first aid kit he'd dug up in the family garden only made that sound when someone far away needed help. Sometimes, Ranger heard the sound when a person was missing or in trouble. Sometimes, he heard it when someone needed Ranger to guide them through a long, dangerous journey.

He pawed through his blanket until he uncovered the old metal box. Beside it was a strange pile of treasures — a quilt square, an odd-shaped leaf, a feather, a broken metal brooch. They were gifts from the children he'd met and helped, all those other times the box had made the sound.

Now it was humming again.

Ranger nuzzled the worn leather strap over his neck. The metal grew warm at his throat. Light began to spill from the cracks in the old box. The humming grew louder and louder. Ranger's skin prickled under his fur. The light grew brighter until he couldn't see his dog bed or the mudroom anymore. Ranger felt as if he were being squeezed through a hole in the sky. The white-hot light was so bright he had to close his eyes.

Finally, the hot metal cooled and the humming stopped. Ranger opened his eyes.

He was standing on a street made of stones. All up and down the block, wooden and brick buildings tipped lopsided. Some were half knocked over.

Ranger sniffed the air. It smelled of bricks and dust and bread.

Then the loose stones began to jump. The buildings lurched and trembled. The vibrations rattled Ranger from his paws to the tips of his ears. What was happening? What was this strange, unsteady place?

"It's starting again!" someone shouted.

"Outside! Quickly!" a voice called from the doorway of one of the brick houses. A crowd of girls poured out. The taller girls pulled the smaller ones close and hurried them away from the rattling building. They huddled together in the street. Then one of the girls broke away from the group and raced back into the building.

A second after she disappeared inside, an upstairs window shattered. Jagged shards of glass rained down on the street. A bit of roofing swung dangerously from the top floor. Bricks from the porch shook loose and tumbled to the sidewalk. The cobblestones kept trembling under Ranger's paws.

This whole strange place was rattling itself to pieces. How was Ranger supposed to help? He couldn't stop the earth from shaking. At least the people in the street were out of the path of the falling glass and bricks. They were safe for now. But none of them had seemed to notice the girl who ran inside . . .

The house rattled and groaned as if it might crumble to the earth at any second. Why hadn't she come back out where it was safer?

Another upstairs window broke and smashed to the sidewalk below.

Ranger bounded up the dusty porch steps and raced inside.

Chapter 3

SHAKING STAIRS
AND FALLING BRICKS

Ranger stepped carefully through the kitchen. Pots and pans and bricks littered the floor. Broken plates, bowls, and teacups spilled from a toppled cupboard. The girl wasn't here.

Ranger had practiced finding people in the rubble of torn-down buildings. But never one that was shaking all around him. He made his way through the mess to the staircase. Shards of shattered glass danced down the rattling stairs. Step by step, Ranger climbed until he reached the top.

The trembling finally stopped, but a big piece of furniture blocked Ranger's way. He climbed up on it with his front paws.

There!

The girl knelt in the middle of the hall. She was hunched over, crying into her gently cupped hands.

Ranger barked.

The girl looked up, her eyes wide with surprise. "Oh!"

Ranger made his way over the fallen cabinet to her side.

Tears streaked down her cheeks. "I left him here," she whispered, and held up her hands. A limp little goldfish, all covered in dust, rested in her palms. "Gum Gum was all right after the first quake. I was so thankful for the good fortune. But then I left him."

Ranger didn't understand what the girl was saying. But he understood sadness. Ranger remembered when Sadie's hermit crab had died last summer. The whole family had gone to the garden to bury it near the roses. Sadie had cried and cried. Ranger had stayed close to her, licking her hand once in a while to remind her he was there.

Ranger sat down beside the girl with the dusty fish. He nuzzled her shoulder with his nose. She laid the fish gently in the puddle on the floor and wrapped her arms around Ranger's neck.

Something creaked and thudded above them. Plaster rained down from the ceiling.

Ranger's skin prickled. The trembling might have stopped, but the house wasn't safe.

Ranger barked. He nudged the girl until she stood up. Then he leaned against her and pushed her toward the stairs. She hesitated, looking back at the little fish.

Ranger barked again, and she seemed to

wake from her daze. She scrambled over the cabinet and started down the steps with Ranger at her side.

The house groaned, and a huge timber crashed through the ceiling into the hallway behind them. A cloud of dust blasted down the stairway. Lily stumbled down the last few steps and fell onto her knees at the bottom of the stairs. Ranger nudged her to her feet. He felt her shaky hand on his collar as he led her through the kitchen and back outside.

"There you are!" called an older woman in a long black dress. "Thank the Lord you're safe."

Lily nodded. Her insides were too churned up to let her speak. She stared at the tilted, battered buildings all up and down the hill. People streamed into the street. Some crawled out their broken windows onto the sidewalk. Many were still barefoot, in nightclothes.

Others had put on all of their best outfits in layers, from their Sunday shoes to their Easter hats. Cats raced like shadows into the alleys. Dogs crouched low with their tails drawn in, scooting over the ground in a panic.

The whole city swarmed like an anthill someone had stirred up with a stick.

A parade of frazzled neighbors had already started up the hill. Families filled the street, carrying bundles of clothes and food over their shoulders. Some trudged along with heavy baskets. Others pulled trunks with thick ropes over the cobblestones.

"You must stay together as we walk to the church," Lo Mo said as she lined the girls up. Lily found the bundle of clothes and food she'd dropped in the street when she ran back inside.

She looked up at the house. Poor Gum

Gum. She hadn't even been able to give him a proper good-bye.

"Come now," Lo Mo said. "Quickly."

Lily picked up her bundle and fell into line. Ranger stayed at her side, and they began the long march up the Sacramento Street hill. The girls walked quietly, lugging the few things they'd had time to grab. Some of the younger children were crying.

"Hush now," Lily whispered as they walked. But with every step, the lump in her throat grew bigger. She tried to be brave and cheerful for the little ones. "It will be all right. You'll see."

Lily looked down at the shaggy dog trotting beside her. It hadn't left her side since it found her in the crumbling hallway upstairs. Maybe the golden dog was Gum Gum's spirit looking after her now. Or maybe it was just a neighborhood stray, scared like all the rest. And what was the strange box it wore around its neck? Lily squinted at the faded lettering on the metal. It was a first aid kit. Someone must have given it to the dog to carry as they fled.

Lily looked around, but she couldn't see an owner. Wherever the dog had come from, Lily was thankful. The feeling of its warm, solid body under her trembling hand was the only thing that kept her moving through the torn-up streets.

Chapter 4

INTO THE SMOKE

The streets teemed with people pushing baby carriages and wagons and wheelbarrows, all piled with their things. Lily passed a man pushing an entire sofa heaped with his belongings. He'd mounted roller skates on the sofa's legs so it would roll. His face was red and sweaty as he huffed and puffed his way up the steep hill. For once, Lily was thankful that she had few possessions to her name.

Others who had come on the steamer to America had extra clothing and gifts from their loved ones. But Lily had arrived for the

month-long journey with only a small basket. It held her bedding, shoes, and a few biscuits. At night, she'd slept on a canvas bunk in the ship's hot, stuffy hold. She'd spent her days searching the sea for spouting whales and practicing the story she would tell immigration officials when she arrived. America had a strict law banning most Chinese immigrants. Lily's family had sent her with phony papers that said she was the child of a merchant, so she was allowed to come.

But that was all a lie. Her parents had sold her as a servant. They simply didn't have enough money to feed Lily and her younger brothers, so they sent her off, hoping she might find a better life across the sea. When the ship docked in San Francisco, officers searched Lily and loaded her onto a cart with the other "paper daughters" who had come ashore. As the cart rolled through the streets, people began throwing litter at the wagon. They shouted at the newly arrived children to go home.

Lily wished she could have. Instead, she moved into the house of a wealthy Chinatown merchant who beat her when she didn't work quickly enough. Lily stayed there four years, until the night Lo Mo came crashing through the door with the police and brought Lily to the mission house.

Lily lived with Lo Mo and the other girls and women now. Lo Mo taught the girls to cook and sew and clean — all the skills that would train them to be good wives. But Lo Mo wasn't interested in Lily's real dream — going to school so she could become a doctor one day. Lily knew that wasn't likely. A Chinese woman might become a teacher, but not a doctor. Still, Lily couldn't stop thinking about the possibility. She'd heard Lo Mo talking about

Elizabeth Blackwell with the churchwomen once. Elizabeth had been the first woman to receive a medical degree in America, and now there were schools for other women, too. Lily had asked Lo Mo about them. Lo Mo shushed her and handed her a broom.

Lily sighed and wiped the sweat from her brow. Her dream seemed further away than ever, with the city crumbling to pieces around her.

Ranger walked beside Lily as the girls trudged up the hill. He was glad the earth had stopped shaking. But the sidewalks were heaped with bricks and splintered wood. He was crossing a buckled street when his paw came down on a shard of broken glass.

Ranger yelped.

"What is it, dog?" Lily looked down. "Are you tired? It's a steep hill."

Ranger tried to keep going. He knew Lily

should stay with her group. But with every step, the glass poked deeper into his paw.

Ranger whimpered, and Lily looked down again.

"You're limping! Let me see . . ." Lily stopped and knelt beside Ranger. She lifted his paw. "Oh, you poor thing! Here . . ." She used the tips of her fingernails to ease the glass from Ranger's paw. "It's out now," Lily said, "but it might still be hard for you to walk. I'll carry that."

Lily lifted the first aid kit from around Ranger's neck. She knelt down, untied her bundle of bedding and clothes, and tucked Ranger's first aid kit inside. Then she stood, ready to catch up to the others.

But Lo Mo and the girls were gone. Lily couldn't spot anyone she knew in the crowd surging up the hill.

"It's all right. We'll find them. We won't be

on our own for long." Lily said the words aloud, trying to convince herself. Lo Mo had told Lily the cruel merchant would try to steal her back if she ever left the house alone. Lily's heart raced.

As she started up the hill again, a frantic, frightened voice rose out of the crowd.

"Father! Father!"

Lily searched the crowd and gasped. "May!" she shouted and held her hand high so the other girl could see her.

May Wong was the daughter of a Chinese grocer. When Lily had been a servant, she'd rarely left the house. But one time, she'd been sent to the Wongs' market for vegetables when her master was ill. She'd met May that day and watched for her out the window ever since.

Lily always envied May, who passed by in the mornings with her arms full of schoolbooks. May was one of the few girls who went to the Chinese Primary School. Her parents believed that girls should be educated as well as boys, so May went along with her little brother, Lee.

But today, May was alone. She ran to Lily. "Father left with Mother to try and find a cart because she can't walk through this mess with her bound feet. He told us to meet them up at Van Ness, but my brother ran back into the shop for water and" — May swallowed hard and took a gasping breath — "the roof collapsed! I called for Little Brother, but he didn't answer. I have to find Father!"

Lily stood up tall and looked over the pulsing crowd. Even if May's father were close by, they'd never find him in the mob. He couldn't help.

But Lily could.

She'd left Gum Gum behind, but that

wouldn't happen again. It couldn't happen. Not to May's little brother.

"I'll go back with you," Lily said, grabbing May's hand. "We'll find him. Come on!"

They turned and hurried back down the block.

Ranger hesitated. The air was thick with dust and smoke and fear. That wasn't where the other girls from the house had gone. It didn't feel safe.

But Ranger felt an unmistakable tug. With Lily was where he needed to be. So he bounded off after her down the hill.

Chapter 5

BURIED ALIVE

Lily and May raced down the hill as quickly as they could, stumbling over loose stones and fallen bricks. They weaved through families with bundles over their shoulders and climbed over twisted streetcar tracks. Shattered glass crunched under their shoes.

When they reached the Wong family's small grocery store, Lily stopped and gasped. The fruit stands in front of the building had collapsed. Oranges and melons spilled down the sidewalk. The store was a heap of beams and bricks and dust.

"Little Brother!" May screamed into the rubble. She whirled to face Lily. "I don't know what to do! He was inside when the roof crumpled into the store. I wanted to go search for him, but I was afraid I'd make something else collapse. He's in there somewhere, though! We have to find him!"

Find!

Ranger stepped carefully through the vegetables and fruits. He'd practiced this kind of search during his training with Luke and Dad. They'd gone to an old building foundation piled with wooden pallets, big pipes, and logs. Luke had hidden in one of the pipes until Ranger searched through the mess to find him. When Ranger found Luke, he barked to give the alert. *Someone is here! Someone needs help!*

Ranger stepped carefully up on the fallen door. It was tippy, but he'd trained to search over all kinds of shaky surfaces. He'd practiced climbing up and down ladders and over loose boards. He'd learned to walk up a teeter-totter, balance in the middle, and walk down the other side.

Ranger walked up the tilted door and climbed over the rubble. Paw by careful paw, he made his way through collapsed shelves and heaps of cans. Sacks of rice had burst open and spilled over the dusty floor. Ranger climbed over a fallen ceiling beam into a more open space and sniffed.

The air was filled with smells. Dried fish. Earthy mushrooms. Vegetables left in the sun.

Finally . . . *There!* From under a heap of boards, Ranger caught the scent of a person. A person who wasn't Lily or May. A person who smelled of oranges and sweat and fear.

Ranger barked.

"What is it?" May's voice was full of hope. "Did he find him?"

"Careful!" Lily said as May started to climb over the timbers and bricks.

Ranger barked again. The crisscrossed boards were scattering the person's scent, but someone was here. Ranger was sure. He pawed at the boards until Lily and May found their way through the rubble.

"Little Brother, I'm here! Are you all right?" May called.

Lily bent low and listened. A weak voice called back from under the rubble. "I'm here . . ."

"We need to get him out!" May grabbed a board and heaved it off the pile into a corner.

Lily flung brick after brick from the heap until a small, dirty hand poked out from an opening.

"Lee!" Lily cried. "Hold on . . . We're going to get you out!"

Ranger stood waiting, watching out for flying bricks until the girls uncovered May's brother. But his legs were still pinned under a heavy shelf that had fallen from the wall. And his eyes were closed.

"Little Brother!" May cried. His eyes fluttered open, but he looked too exhausted to speak. "Stay with me. You're almost free . . ." May said, and bent to lift the shelf. It didn't budge. "Hold on. It's going to be all right."

May turned to Lily in tears and whispered, "It's too heavy!"

"We can do it together," Lily said. "We don't have to lift it all the way — just enough so he can wiggle free."

Lily squatted and curled her hands under the splintered edge of the shelving. "Get that corner," she told May. "We'll lift together on the count of three. Ready?"

May lowered herself into place and nodded.

"One . . . two . . . three!" Lily braced her feet on the floor and pushed up with her legs as hard as she could. The shelving was sturdy and thick. The edge of the wood cut into her palms. Lily pushed harder with her legs. She heard May grunting from the effort. Finally, they lifted the shelf high enough to free Lee's legs.

"Hurry, Little Brother!" May said. Her voice shook under the weight. "Tell us when you're out!"

Lily's arms trembled. She didn't know how much longer she could hold on. Lee didn't answer May. Was he out yet?

Lily looked down. Lee hadn't moved at all. "Lee!" she shouted. "Lee!"

His eyes were closed.

"Oh no . . . no . . ." May's voice trembled.

Lily felt the shelf get heavier in her hands. "May, hold on!" she cried.

Ranger barked.

Lily staggered under the weight of the wood. "Go get him, dog! Please! Go on! Get him up!"

Ranger jumped over the edge of the shelves and crouched at Lee's side. He barked again, but the boy didn't open his eyes. Sometimes Luke didn't like to get up in the morning when it was time for school. When he slept through his noisy alarm clock, Ranger would jump on his bed and lick him awake. This wasn't the same, Ranger could tell. This boy was hurt. But he had to wake up to get to safety, so Ranger barked again. Then he bent down and licked the boy's face until his eyes opened.

"Pull yourself out!" May shouted. "Hurry!"

The boy's eyes grew wide. He rose onto his elbows, but his face twisted in pain, and he fell back. "I can't." He gasped. "It hurts. I can't move."

"You have to!" Lily cried. She didn't think she could hold on much longer.

Chapter 6

NOWHERE TO TURN

May's voice broke. "You can do it, Little Brother. Please . . ."

Ranger pawed at the boy's shoulder.

Lee lifted himself onto his elbows again and grimaced. He took a deep, shaking breath and pulled himself backward a few inches.

"Yes!" May was crying now. "Keep going . . . please . . ."

Lee squeezed his eyes closed and clenched his teeth. Inch by inch, he dragged himself out from under the shelves.

"He's clear!" Lily said, finally letting out

her breath. They let go and the shelf thudded to the floor. Lily's hands throbbed. She didn't think she could have held on a moment longer.

The girls rushed to Lee's side. His face was pale and gray as smoke. One of his legs was twisted at an unnatural angle. When Lily bent to touch it, Lee cried out.

"I think his leg is broken," Lily said. "He needs a doctor."

"We have a small wagon in the back," May said. "Father uses it to bring goods from the harbor. I'll fetch it and we can take him to the dispensary."

Lily nodded. "We'll need a way to keep his leg steady if we're going to move him. I don't want to make it worse." She searched out a thin board from one of the broken shelves. While May went to find the wagon, Lily took the sheet from her bundle of bedding. She put the board up against Lee's leg and, as slowly as she could, eased the sheet underneath to wrap it tight.

Ranger sat close to the boy, leaning against him as Lily worked. Still, Lee cried out in pain every time she touched his leg.

When May returned, they eased one of Mr. Wong's jackets underneath Lee and used it to lift him into the wagon.

Slowly, Lily and May hauled the wagon out of the shop and down the uneven street. Every time they tried to go more quickly, the wagon hit a bump, and Lee cried out again.

Finally, they reached the Tung Wah Dispensary, the only place for medical care in Chinatown. Lily and May pulled the wagon up to the door, but no one came when they knocked.

"They've all gone up to Van Ness," said a man rushing down the street. "Try Central

Emergency Hospital at City Hall." Then he continued on his way.

"I know where that is," May said. "I went to City Hall with Father once to deliver some papers." She pointed up toward Market Street, where new clouds of smoke were rising into the purple sky.

Lily took a deep breath. She nodded and picked up the handle of Lee's wagon. "Let's go."

Lee moaned as the wagon bounced over the cobblestones, all the way down Stockton Street. Lily's heart felt as if it might break in two every time he cried. It was a blessing when he finally passed out.

Market Street teemed with people, but none of them offered help. Women in dresses and Sunday hats and men in suits rushed along toward the ferry landing.

The air swirled with smoke, dust, and wild

rumors. Some people said the earthquake had shaken America all the way from the Atlantic to the Pacific! There were reports of a tidal wave in Chicago, and one man claimed that Salt Lake City had simply disappeared. Lily wondered if the whole world might be ending.

Snapped power lines lay in the street, twisting and hissing like snakes. Whole faces were ripped off homes. Lily could look inside the rooms as if she were peering into a dollhouse.

For nearly an hour, Ranger walked beside the wagon as they made their way through the crumbling city. The wagon thumped over another ridge, and Ranger heard his first aid kit clunk against something else in Lily's bundle. He wondered when he would get to go home.

He'd found Lily in the shaking, crumbling house. He'd gone with her to save Lee. But the old metal box wasn't humming yet. That meant Ranger's work wasn't finished. Looking around this smoky, fear-filled place, he worried it might be a long time before he saw Luke and Sadie again.

"It's just up here," May said. "Right — oh!"

Lily stopped and stared. The earthquake had shaken the stones off City Hall's grand tower. Only the metal frame remained. It looked to Lily as if a whisper of wind might knock it to the ground. Bricks lay piled in dusty heaps all around the building. Chunks of broken columns were everywhere.

"It's in ruins!" Lily cried. She rushed up to a soldier on a horse. "Please . . . where are the doctors from the hospital?" she asked. "My friend's brother is hurt."

The man lifted his chin toward a nearby building. "They've moved everyone to Mechanics' Pavilion."

Lily and May started off again, pulling the wagon, with Ranger at their side. The streets were littered with twisted rails and fallen stonework. Every few steps, they'd have to lift the wagon over a crack or wheel it around a slab of broken concrete.

Lee had woken up and was moaning again. Lily paused and put a hand on his pale forehead. It was cold and clammy. His breathing was shallow and fast. All around them, the distant smoke seemed to be closing in. Were the fires getting closer?

Lily said a quiet prayer that the doctors the soldier had promised would still be at the pavilion when they arrived. *Please let there be room for him,* Lily thought. *And please let the doctors be willing to help.*

Chapter 7

WHO'S THE DOCTOR?

Lily and May weren't the only ones looking for help. Horses, carts, and carriages clogged the entrance to the pavilion, waiting to drop off the injured.

Ranger stayed close to the girls as they pulled Lee's wagon through the crowd. This new place felt too smoky and crowded to be safe. Whenever Lily and May paused, Ranger stepped up to the wagon and nuzzled Lee's hand. Sometimes, the boy stirred and put his hand on Ranger's head. But more and more often, he didn't even seem to notice.

"Over here," Lily said. They pulled the wagon inside, and she gasped.

The wooden building swarmed with doctors and nurses. Red Cross women rushed along with carts of supplies. Hundreds of mattresses crowded the floor, all full of people hurting. Some had burns from the fires. Others had head injuries and broken bones. Maybe they'd been trapped like Lee.

"Excuse me . . ." May called out to a nurse rushing past, but her voice got lost in the chaos. Ranger raced in front of the nurse and barked.

The nurse whirled around. "Whose dog is this?"

"Please . . ." Lily rushed up to the woman. "My friend's brother is hurt. I think his leg is broken, and his breathing is all strange and shallow."

The nurse's face softened, and she seemed

to forget about Ranger. She knelt beside Lee and put a hand on his forehead. Then she picked up his wrist and held it for a moment. "He's in shock," she said, and looked around.

Nearby, two men were lifting a skinny man from one of the mattresses. His body was limp. As they carried him to a corner of the building, the nurse pointed to the empty space. "Come along with me."

They lifted Lee onto the mattress and covered him with a wool blanket. "We need to keep him warm until a doctor is free to tend to his leg," the nurse said. "Who made this splint?"

"I did." Lily looked down. Poor Lee had been bounced halfway through the city with her messy work barely holding his leg in place. She'd done a terrible job and waited for the nurse to tell her so.

"You did a fine job," the nurse said quietly.

"I can tell you didn't have much to work with, but you kept the bone in place. Stay with him for now. I'll send a doctor when I can." And she hurried off into the crowd.

Soon, a woman in a long, dark dress walked up to Lee's mattress. "I understand your brother's leg is broken," she said.

"Yes," May said. "Another nurse already sent for a doctor. We're waiting for him."

"For *her*," the woman said. She knelt beside the mattress, opened a small leather bag, and pulled out a stethoscope. "I'm the doctor. Tell me what happened."

Lily stared for a moment.

"How was he hurt?" the doctor asked again.

Lily snapped out of her wondering. "He was trapped when the market roof caved in."

The doctor nodded. She pressed the end of the stethoscope to Lee's chest and listened.

"Is he all right?" May asked.

"I think he will be," the doctor said. She pulled back the blanket and gently unwrapped the sheet that held Lily's splint in place. With a sharp knife, she cut off Lee's cotton shoe and sliced his trouser leg up the seam. "I'm going to straighten your leg now," she said quietly.

Lee cried out in pain, and Lily had to look away. Her eyes burned with tears, and the mattresses and hurrying people all blurred together.

Finally, the doctor said, "All right. I've set the bone, splinted it, and given him something to help him rest. Once the fires are under control, we'll see about moving to a proper hospital." She sighed, and Lily could tell she wasn't sure when that might happen.

"Thank you," May said. The doctor nodded and hurried off to another patient.

May turned to Lily then. "And thank *you*," she said. "If you hadn't helped, I . . ." She shook

her head and pressed her lips together. "But you probably need to go. Won't someone be looking for you?"

"Probably." Lily hesitated, not sure how much May knew about her. "I live at the mission house now. Lo Mo has fifty girls, so she won't have time to worry much about me. I'll stay with you to keep your brother company."

"I'd like that," May said. She looked down at Lee, sleeping now, and stroked his wispy black hair. Then she looked back up at Lily. "You must miss your family. I mean . . . you have a new family at the house with —"

"Not really," Lily said. "We're cared for, but . . ." It was hard to explain. Lily's memories of her real family had faded in the years since she left China. But the hole in her heart was still there. She reached down to pet the fluffy golden dog that seemed to have adopted her. It was the closest thing to a friend she'd had in a long time. May was starting to feel like a friend, too. Lily didn't want to think about leaving her and going back to the mission house.

Ranger was glad to be out of the busy, dusty streets. His paws were sore, and he was tired. He leaned into Lily's hand and closed his eyes. But then he caught a scent that made his nose twitch.

Ranger sat up straight and sniffed the musty pavilion air. It smelled of blood and sweat and ... *smoke!* Stronger and thicker than before. The fire was closer than it had been. Ranger looked around, but no one seemed concerned.

"What's the matter, dog?" Lily said, staring at him.

Ranger left her. He hurried up and down the rows of mattresses until he found where the smoke was strongest. Then he barked and barked until he was surrounded by doctors and nurses. Finally, someone shouted over the crowd.

"The roof is on fire!"

Chapter 8

RACING THE FLAMES

Panic filled the pavilion.

"Where is it?"

"Find a ladder!"

"Get it out!"

Doctors and nurses raced up and down the rows of mattresses. They clustered in little groups, wringing their hands. They pointed up at the rafters, then looked around at the hundreds of people who would never be able to save themselves if the fire spread.

"Should we try to get him back in the wagon?" May said.

Lily looked down at Lee, finally resting after his painful, bumpy ride through the city. She couldn't imagine waking him and hurting him again. But if it was the only way to save him from the flames, then —

"It's out! They put it out!" someone shouted.

Lily's heart unclenched. Thank goodness they didn't have to make that awful choice.

The roar of the building subsided, and a nurse came by to check on Lee.

"His pulse is nearly back to normal," she said, and smiled at Lily and May. "That's good news."

"And it's safe now, so we don't have to move him?" Lily asked, just to be certain.

"For now," the nurse said. "One of the policemen got up in the crossbeams and was able to put out the fire, but . . ." She glanced up at the ceiling.

"But what?" May said.

The nurse shook her head quickly. "The sky is full of embers, and the fire's still spreading." She tucked Lee's blanket around him and stood up. "But we'll face that if it comes."

Lily swallowed hard. "Thank you."

After the nurse left, the girls sat on the floor beside Lee. Ranger flopped down next to them.

"I never knew you had a dog at the mission house," May said.

"We didn't." Lily leaned over to scratch Ranger's ear. "He showed up this morning after the quake. He came after me when the beams started falling. I'd gone back into the house to try and save our goldfish." She looked down.

"I'm sorry," May said quietly. She reached over and patted Ranger's head. "We had a canary when we first arrived. He used to sing in his corner of the store when I came home from school."

Lily swallowed hard and looked up. "What's it like there?"

"School?" May looked surprised. "Well, the teacher is strict, and she —"

Someone near the door shouted, and two policemen burst into the building.

May's mouth hung open with her unfinished thought. "What's happening?"

A nurse ran past them. "Come with me!" she called and motioned for them to follow. "The fire's returned!" she called over her shoulder. "Dr. Millar has ordered the building evacuated. We need every able-bodied person to help!"

"What about my brother?" May shouted after the nurse.

"We'll get him out. But you must come with me now."

May hesitated, and Lily understood why. Lee looked so small and crumpled on the mattress. How could they leave him?

But they had no choice. "We must do as she says, May. We'll hurry. We'll come back for him soon. Until then, the dog can watch over him." Lily looked down at Ranger. "Stay," she said firmly. "Stay with him. We'll come back. Stay."

Ranger understood *stay*. He sat beside Lee's mattress and watched the girls rush after the nurse. The smoke was getting thicker.

Ranger stayed by the boy's side. His first aid kit was wrapped up in Lily's bedding, still quiet. But the whole building buzzed with rushing fear. All around him, people were shouting and crying. A woman hurried by with a tiny baby in her arms. Another man limped along, dragging a child on a mattress behind him. Ranger had helped people who were injured before. He'd seen people hurting — but never so, so many at once. How could he possibly help them all?

Lily and May followed the nurse to the big doors that led to the street. The aisles were clogged with people dragging patients on their mattresses. Outside, men flagged down automobiles and horse-drawn carts. The entrance was packed with waiting vehicles.

"Over here!" a man called to them. Lily and May followed the nurse to his side, where a short, plump woman lay passed out on a mattress near a waiting cart. Her head was wrapped with bandages, and her hands were scratched and burned. "We need three on each side to load her in. Come now," the man said.

Lily and May stood next to the man on one side of the mattress, while the nurse and two other men squatted down across from them. "On three now," the man said, and counted, "One, two, three!" They clasped hands under the sagging mattress, lifted it up, and shuffled along until they reached the wagon. Then they loaded the woman in, mattress and all.

The nurse pointed them toward another mattress. Those closest to the doors had to be moved first to make room for others, like Lee, who were stuck in the middle of the building.

Lily coughed on the thickening smoke and looked back into the churning sea of people.

How quickly were the flames spreading? Would there be enough carts and automobiles to move everyone? And would there be time?

They were racing the fire now. And there was no way to tell who would win.

Chapter 9

INTO THE FIRE

Lily and May helped load patient after patient into waiting carts. Smoke burned Lily's eyes, but she pushed through the crowd and led May back to the spot where Lee rested on his mattress on the floor.

Ranger stood up and barked. He was happy the girls were back! But they didn't stop to pet him or scratch his ear.

"Put our things on the mattress," Lily said. "We'll have to leave the wagon."

May grabbed her father's jacket from the wagon, shook it out, and bundled up the few things she'd grabbed on her way out of the store. She tucked it beside Lee, along with Lily's bundle of bedding and clothing from the home.

"Ready?" Lily said. She and May squatted side by side, grabbed the end of Lee's mattress, and dragged it into the mass of people rushing for the doors.

The noise in the huge building grew louder by the minute. Even with two of them pulling, the mattress was heavy. Lily's cotton shoes slipped on the dust-covered floor. Ranger walked behind them.

As they reached the doors, another automobile pulled up. A man jumped out of the driver's seat.

Lily ran to him. "Thank you so much for stopping! My friend's brother needs to be taken —"

"Not in *my* automobile," the man barked, and pushed Lily aside.

Ranger crouched low and growled. But the man didn't come near Lily again. He rushed past her to help lift a white man's mattress into the back of his car, and drove away.

"Bring him here!" someone called. Lily turned and saw the lady doctor who had treated Lee before. She was holding open the back of a cart, already loaded with two mattresses spilling over each other. "Load him in. You won't be able to ride with him, but you can walk up and find him. I believe they're being taken to the emergency hospital at Golden Gate Park."

Lily and May pulled their bundles off the mattress. They crouched beside the doctor and three Red Cross workers, clasped hands under Lee's mattress, and hoisted him into the cart.

"All right now!" the doctor called to the driver, and his horse trotted away, up the street.

Lily hugged her bundle to her chest. She watched until Lee's cart was swallowed up in the crowd.

Finally, May tugged at her sleeve. "Let's head for the park."

Ranger trotted beside the girls and nudged them along when they slowed down. The air was still thick with smoke and fear. He wanted to get them to safety, back with their people. Maybe then he could finally go home, too.

The streets were filled with even more refugees now, fleeing from fires that spread through the city. Everyone was talking about what the flames had already devoured and where they were headed next. The sea of people moved in a giant wave up Market Street. But every so often, Lily and May passed men running against the crowd, back into the flames.

"Aa baak, what are you doing?" Lily called out to an older Chinese man who'd slowed to climb over some twisted streetcar rails. "The fires are spreading that way. There's shelter up at the parks."

"Fires will be in Chinatown soon," the man said. "I must save my family's papers." And he rushed off.

May grabbed Lily's arm. Her eyes were huge. "Our papers!" she said. "Father told me to bring them, but when Lee was hurt — oh!" Her face crumpled.

"It will be all right," Lily said. But she knew that was a lie. American laws forced Chinese people to carry papers wherever they went. At any time, officials could stop you and ask to see them. If you didn't have them — if you'd left them at home or lost them — you could be sent away forever. Lo Mo kept all of her girls' papers and the documents that gave her custody. Lily was sure she must have taken them when they left the mission house. But the whole Wong family would be in trouble without the documents that proved they were allowed to be here. Documents that May was supposed to have saved for them — and didn't.

May clung to Lily's hand. "I have to go back," she said. "I can't let — I have to go."

Lily looked into the blackened sky behind them. She wanted to run from the billowing clouds.

But she couldn't let May go alone. She squeezed May's hand. "I'll come with you."

Together, they ran back down Market Street, into the smoke and ash.

Chapter 10

CHAOS AND CANARIES

Lily, May, and Ranger hurried back toward Chinatown. They weaved through crowds of people, all rushing the other way, away from the spreading fires.

Lily's throat burned from the smoke. She wished she'd thought to bring water from the pavilion, but all she had in her bundle was a bit of bread from breakfast. Was it really just this morning that the earth had shaken her awake? So much had happened since she'd slipped away from the mission house girls as

they marched up the hill. Lily fished out the bread and broke off pieces for May and Ranger.

They ate as they walked through the crowd. Hundreds of quiet, tired people surged toward the ferries, carrying what they could. Some had wrapped their things in bedclothes like Lily had. Others looked as if they'd simply grabbed whatever they found on their way out the door. Lily saw three people pass by with canaries and one with an empty cage. Lily wondered what happened to the bird. Maybe it had flown into the cool woods or off over the bay.

Along with the refugees, there were more and more soldiers in the streets. They galloped by on horses and stood guard in front of crumbling buildings, holding long rifles at their sides. Troops were clearing bricks and stone from the streets. They stopped practically all the men who passed by to work with them.

But the soldiers ignored May and Lily until they tried to turn down one of the side streets.

"Area's closed off," a soldier said. He towered over them on his horse.

May looked up at him. "I must get our papers. We live just down the street, and —"

The soldier lifted his gun. "Doesn't matter where you live. They're getting ready to dynamite buildings to stop the fire. No one's going in."

"They're blowing up our homes?" May's eyes were huge. "They can't! I have to —"

"May, we have to go." Lily tugged her friend's arm and pulled her away, with Ranger at their side. Lily couldn't imagine how awful it must feel to have a home and know it was about to be destroyed. She knew how much May's family needed those papers. But she also knew that arguing with the soldier would only make things worse.

"Maybe there's another way in," Lily whispered. "But we'll have to be fast." They backtracked until they found an open street that led toward the Wong family's grocery store.

"How can blowing up buildings stop the fire?" May said as they rushed down the side street.

"I'm not sure," Lily said. But she'd been watching the fires in the distance. They seemed to spread as if by magic. As if the flames could leap across streets from one building to another on the far side. "Maybe by creating space between buildings so the flames have nowhere to go."

But so far, the fire was winning. More and more people filled the streets, fleeing from the burned districts in groups of two or three or four. Lily caught bits of their conversations as they hurried past.

"No time to go back for the silver . . ."

"Send word to Uncle Jacob in Oakland . . ."

". . . water and food at the park . . ."

Then a voice rose louder than the rest. "Canaries! Free! Can you take a bird?"

Lily spun around and saw a short, bald man in a doorway on the far side of the street. He held a cage out toward the sidewalk. Inside was a tiny golden bird.

"Oh!" Lily gasped. She felt as if she'd finally glimpsed the sun, shining through this dark afternoon. She left May and ran to the man. "We can't, but . . . You're giving them away?"

The man nodded sadly. "Just got a big shipment in, and the fire's heading this way. There's no way I'll be able to save them all. I'd rather let them go than have them perish."

"Lily, come on!" May called from the street.

"Can you take one?" The man held out the bamboo cage.

The bird gave a little hop on its perch. Its tail feathers trembled.

"Do you sing?" Lily said, and whistled a few notes. The bird didn't sing back. It looked out at Lily with scared black eyes.

I can't, Lily thought. Not with all they had to carry. Not with the fire spreading and papers to save and still so far to go. But the bird's bright feathers reminded her of Gum Gum's shining golden scales, and her eyes burned. *No,* she thought.

"Yes," she said. She took the cage and hurried back to May.

"Lily!" May said. "What —"

"He was going to be left behind," she said quietly. "I couldn't leave him."

"But . . ." May started to say something but stopped. "Let's go. It's not far."

The crowd thinned, and soon they reached the Wongs' street. But another soldier on horseback stood guard at the top of the block. He held up a hand when the girls started toward him.

"No one's allowed in the area," he barked. "The mayor issued an order. Anyone stealing or looting is to be shot on sight."

"We're not looting," Lily blurted.

"I live here," May said. "And I have to —"

"No exceptions," the soldier said.

Lily stared past him. She could see the Wongs' store. It was so close.

"Please . . ." May stepped toward the officer.

Lily pulled her back. "We understand, sir," Lily said, and hustled May around the corner.

"What do you mean, we understand?" May cried. Tears made trails down her dusty cheeks. "Without those papers —"

"You can't force your way past the army," Lily said. "But I have another idea."

Chapter 11

COUNTDOWN TO DYNAMITE

Lily huddled with May in the doorway of a nearby laundry. "Is there a back way into your family's apartment?" she asked.

May shook her head. "It's just a single room behind the store. There's a window, but I'm not sure I'd fit. What if the back alley is guarded?"

"We can check." Lily slipped out from the doorway and ducked into the alley behind the Wongs' store. A soldier on a horse stood guard at the far end of the street. He was facing the other way.

"Don't make a sound," Lily whispered. She was thankful now that the little canary didn't sing. They slipped from doorway to doorway until they were behind the store.

"All right . . ." May took a deep breath and started across the street.

Lily pulled her back. "You can't just burst out and climb in the window," she whispered. "If that officer sees, he'll think you're breaking in to loot, and with the mayor's order . . ." Lily shook her head. She couldn't say the words aloud.

The only way to make sure the soldier's attention didn't land on May was to give him someone else to worry about. "Let me go down the alley first," Lily said. "I'll approach him asking for help with . . . I don't know. Something. I'll get him turned away so you can go in. Stay hidden until then."

"But what if . . ." May bit her lip. Then she

said, "All right. I'll be very fast. Should we meet back by the laundry?"

Lily nodded. "Be safe." She looked down at Ranger and whispered, "Ready, dog? You're coming with me."

Ranger nuzzled Lily's hand and followed her into the alley. After a few steps, Lily's shoe crunched down on some shards of broken window.

The soldier whirled his horse around. "Area's closed off!" he shouted.

Lily stopped. "Can you help me, please?" she called. "I . . . I thought I saw some men looting shops." She pointed past the soldier, away from the Wongs' store. "I can show you . . ."

The officer frowned. He started toward Lily but then turned back and looked up and down the street. "Come here!" he called.

Lily's heart thumped so hard she felt as if the earth might be shaking again. Ranger

nudged her hand, and they walked to the soldier. Lily stared up at him. "It was up on Stockton."

"Show me." The soldier turned his horse and started up the street. But then glass smashed behind them.

No! May must have knocked the window loose.

The soldier whirled his horse around and started down the alley.

Ranger wasn't sure what to think of this soldier. But he knew May was back there. He knew from all the whispering that she and Lily didn't want anyone to know. But the soldier was riding that way.

Ranger started barking.

The soldier looked over his shoulder. "What's that dog's problem?" He turned back toward the Wongs' store.

Ranger ran up to the corner, barking and growling. He ran back to the soldier and barked again. Back and forth he raced, until Lily said, "Oh! I bet he's seen the looters!" She ran to the corner with Ranger and pointed. "Look!"

The soldier galloped up beside her and narrowed his eyes. "I don't see anyone."

Ranger ran ahead of them and stepped up to the doorway of a restaurant. He growled into the broken-down darkness until the soldier rode up to him and peered into the building, too.

Lily dropped her birdcage and bundle. She pointed into the empty building and prayed the dog would keep barking at the imaginary looters. "Where'd they go, dog?"

Ranger barked into the building. He stepped carefully into the entry. The building smelled of plaster and dust, chicken and grease. There were no men here. But Ranger could hear Lily talking with the soldier outside. "He's a good dog. He'll bark if he finds them."

Ranger stayed inside until he heard horses' hooves on the cobblestones. Was the soldier leaving? Ranger barked. The hooves stopped. Ranger padded out into the smoky afternoon light.

Lily looked up at the soldier and shook her head. "They must have gotten away. Perhaps you should —"

"I will return to my post," the soldier said. "You will leave the area as ordered."

"Of course." Lily gathered her things and started toward the alley.

The soldier pointed up the block. "The other way. Now." He raised his rifle.

Lily and Ranger hurried away. Halfway up the block, Lily stopped and turned to look back. The soldier was gone. He was probably already back at the entrance to the alley. She and the dog had only managed to keep him busy for a few minutes. Had it been long enough for May to get the papers and slip away?

Lily led the dog around the block. She circled back to the laundry where she and May had agreed to meet.

The doorway was empty. The street was littered with bricks and glass as usual, but Ranger spotted something else wedged in the cobblestones. He trotted over and found a tiny cloth doll. Ranger sniffed it. It smelled of cotton and dust and . . . May.

Ranger barked. Lily looked down and picked up the doll. She'd often seen May carrying the little cloth figure on her way to school. Had May left it for her on purpose to let her know she'd continued on to the park to find Lee?

Lily looked up and down the street. May wasn't there. But a new soldier was approaching.

Lily didn't wait to have another gun pointed her way. "Come, dog!" She turned and hurried up the hill. Behind her, a great booming blast shook the city. Had the men started blowing up buildings? Another explosion shook the street, and a cloud of dust filled the sky.

How many would have to be destroyed to stop the fires? Would they dynamite the mission house? The Wongs' store and home? Lily was beginning to wonder if anything would be left of the city when this day finally ended.

Chapter 12

CITY IN THE PARK

Lily plodded up the hill toward Golden Gate Park. The streets weren't as crowded as they'd been earlier, but every so often, Lily passed someone hurrying back toward Chinatown. Maybe they were hoping to save their family's papers, like May. Lily hoped they'd find their way past the soldiers, get what they needed, and stay safe.

Where was May? Lily searched every doorway she passed. Once she got away from Chinatown, the streets grew busier. Families gathered around stoves they'd dragged outside or built out of stones. They fried bacon and stirred pots, watching the fires spread in the distance.

Bacon! Ranger was hungry. Scents of smoked meat and chicken stew mingled with the ash from the fires. All the families gathered around their homemade brick ovens reminded him of cooking out on the patio with Luke and Sadie and their parents. Those fires were full of rich smells and easy laughter, but it wasn't like that now. Here, good scents mingled with other smells — crumbling buildings, bitter smoke, and death. They'd passed several horses that had been crushed under fallen walls. Ranger walked close to Lily, nudging her away from buildings that still seemed to be settling from the quake.

Ranger sniffed at the doll sticking out from

Lily's bundle of clothes. He sniffed again and got so close to Lily that she tripped over his feet.

"What are you doing, dog?" Lily asked. She stopped, took the doll from the sack, and looked at it. Then she held it out to Ranger. "Are you after May's doll?" Ranger sniffed again. "We need to find her. Where is she?" Lily asked.

Find!

Ranger barked. He sniffed at the air and the ground for any other trace of May's scent. But if she'd escaped Chinatown before the blasts began, she hadn't come this way.

After a few blocks, Lily sighed and tucked the doll back into her bundle. She kept watching for May, but there was no sign of her friend. Lily wasn't even sure which direction she was headed anymore. Her eyes burned. Her feet ached. Her hands were cramped and her arms trembled from carrying the birdcage and bundle of clothes so far. Every few blocks, another fire or blocked-off street turned her around. Finally, she found her way back to Market Street and climbed the long hill to Golden Gate Park.

When she arrived, the entire city was there! At least it seemed that way. The army had opened relief stations. Tired-looking people stood in long lines that snaked around buildings and trees.

Lily stepped up to an officer who was watching a line. "Excuse me . . . I'm looking for my friend."

"Ha!" The man laughed and swept his arm out over the mob. "Good luck!"

Lily didn't give up. "She'd be with her brother, I think. And he's hurt. Is there a hospital? Someplace where the injured are being tended?"

The man tipped his head toward the mob. "Hospital tent's over yonder." Then he looked down at Lily. "But they've moved the Chinese to a separate camp at the Presidio." He pointed the other way.

Lily was confused. "But . . . the doctor at Mechanics' Pavilion said —"

"You're not going to find your people here," the soldier said. "You'd best be on your way." And he turned back to the bread line.

Tears stung Lily's eyes. Her stomach ached with hunger, but she took Ranger's collar, whispered, "Come on, dog," and squeezed through the crowd in the direction the officer had pointed. Lily gripped the birdcage so tightly her hand cramped. Every part of her felt angry and clenched. Why wasn't Lee being cared for where the doctor had sent him? What kind of city took the time to sort and separate people when everyone was hurting so much?

Ranger nudged Lily's hand. She ignored him at first, but then he nuzzled again and she stopped for a moment. She put down the birdcage and her bundle of clothes, dropped to her knees beside him, and let herself cry. Ranger leaned against her as she sobbed. Then he licked her cheek.

Lily sniffled and took a deep breath. Then she stood and picked up her things. "We'll find Lee and May at the Presidio," she told Ranger. Her voice sounded certain and true. But she'd never felt more alone in her life.

Chapter 13

FEVER AND FRIENDSHIP

By the time Lily and Ranger reached the Presidio, the sun was low in the smoke-clouded sky. Lily pushed her way through the crowd, past soldiers and trees and tents, until she started to see other Chinese people.

"Aa baak, excuse me," she asked an older man rushing past with a cup of water. "Can you tell me where the emergency hospital is?"

The man pointed down a row of tents that seemed to go on forever.

"Thank you." Lily and Ranger hurried along until they found a larger tent with carts

and horses outside. Two men were carrying another man in through the open flaps. Lily and Ranger ducked in after them.

Lily wasn't sure if dogs would be allowed, but everyone was too busy to notice. Doctors and nurses bent over patients on cots. Volunteers rushed by with bandages, medicine, and water. All the patients looked alike — hurt, bandaged, covered up, and scared. Lily couldn't tell if Lee was here or not. She started toward one of the rows of cots.

Ranger followed Lily, sniffing at the matted-down grass. Things weren't as dusty here, but lots of feet had trampled the earth. He smelled dirt and sweat and blood. And then he caught a quick scent of the May girl who'd dropped her doll.

Ranger stopped and sniffed the air. *There!* He nudged Lily down a row of cots.

"Where are you going?" Lily said. "Do you smell something?"

Ranger tracked the scent to the far side of the tent. Lily trailed after him until she spotted Lee on the very last bed. May knelt beside him.

"You're here!" Lily rushed to May's side and threw her arms around her.

"You came!" May said.

Ranger wagged his tail and sniffed at Lee on the cot. The boy was awake. He looked exhausted, and his cheeks were flushed, but he gave a weak smile when Ranger licked his hand.

"Thank goodness!" May said. "I got the papers, but I couldn't find you when I went back to the laundry. You didn't come, and I was afraid —"

"We did come. You were already gone."

"The soldiers . . ." May's eyes filled with tears.

"It's all right," Lily said. "We're here. Did you find your family?"

May shook her head. "I've looked everywhere, but it's like searching for a needle someone's dropped in the wide open sea." She looked at Lily's pack and smiled, reaching out for the little cloth doll. "You found my doll."

Ranger sniffed at the doll again and barked. He'd found May. He'd done his job, again. But when he poked his nose deeper into Lily's bundle, the first aid kit still felt cool and quiet. When would he get to go home?

"Is this your dog?" a nurse asked. Her eyes landed on the bamboo cage beside Lee's cot. "And bird, too?"

Lily nodded. "I'll take them out soon, but . . . please can we stay for a few minutes? The dog cheers my friend's brother."

The nurse looked down at Lee and smiled a little. But when she put a hand on his forehead, her eyes filled with concern. "He's got a fever," she said. "Has he been treated for infection?"

"I . . . I'm not sure." Lily said. She tried to remember what the doctor had told them back at the pavilion. With the fire and evacuation, it all seemed like a blur.

The nurse looked at May. "Where are your parents?"

"I don't know," she answered.

The nurse knelt beside Lee and curled her fingers around his wrist. She lifted the blanket that covered his legs and pressed her lips together. Then she turned back to May. "I don't want to scare you," she said quietly, "but you need to find your parents."

"I looked for them when I got here, but it's so crowded. Everyone's huddled in the tents. I don't know where to start." May grabbed her father's jacket from the cot and pulled it close.

"We'll find them, May. We will," Lily said. "I

found you, didn't I?" She looked down at Ranger, who was sniffing at May's little doll. "Actually . . . it wasn't me. It was the dog. It sounds odd, but I think he smelled you." She paused for a moment, then took the jacket from May's hand and held it out to Ranger.

Ranger sniffed the woolen fabric.

"That's May's father. Mr. Wong. Smell him?" Lily rubbed the sides of the jacket together and put it right up to Ranger's nose.

Ranger sniffed again. The jacket smelled of dust and smoke. It held Lee's scent and May's and someone else's . . . but that person wasn't here in the hospital tent. Ranger looked up at Lily.

"Stay with your brother. I'll take the dog and go look for him," Lily told May. She didn't want to leave the tent. Not with night falling. Not when she'd felt so alone and finally found her friend. But May couldn't leave Lee by himself. If the soldier was right — if they'd sent all the Chinese refugees to the Presidio — then Mr. Wong had to be here, too.

Lily gazed down at her tiny golden bird in its cage on the floor. "You can watch over Lee while we're gone." She looked up at the nurse. "Is it all right if he stays just for a while? Please?"

She nodded. "Perhaps his song will brighten up this night."

"He doesn't sing," May said.

"Not yet," Lily added. "But maybe someday when things are better."

Lily knelt and looked into the cage. The little canary hopped over to the side, just inches from her nose. It reminded Lily of the way her goldfish used to come to the glass to say hello. She took May's hand and promised, "I'll find your father. I will." Then Lily picked up the jacket and headed back out into the mob.

Chapter 14

NIGHT WITHOUT DARKNESS

Find!

Ranger was good at tracking people by scent. When he was practicing to be a search-and-rescue dog, he'd found Luke in a confusing training area with lots of other scent trails. But that hadn't been nearly as busy as this crowded park. People hurried everywhere, carrying bundles, pushing carriages, pulling suitcases, wagons, and carts.

Ranger sniffed the air as he and Lily walked through the mob. So many smells! He smelled dirt and grass, all trampled and stirred. He smelled horses and birds, fires burning and coffee heating. He smelled lots and lots of people. But so far, he hadn't caught the scent of the jacket man.

Ranger followed Lily through the buzzing crowd. Army men were handing out canvas tents and showing people how to set them up. The tents went on for rows and rows and all looked alike. None of them smelled like the jacket.

Lily's stomach ached with hunger, and her legs were shaky. But she walked with Ranger up and down the rows, calling, "Mr. Wong? Mr. Wong?" Lily tried not to think about Lee's hot face and shallow breaths back at the hospital.

The last of the hazy sunlight disappeared. But it didn't get dark. Flames from the burning city lit the sky. It was bright enough to make out people's faces, even in the shadows. Where was Mr. Wong?

Finally, Ranger paused outside one of the tents. His ears pricked up. He held his tail still and sniffed.

There!

Ranger barked.

"What is it, dog?" Lily stopped beside the tent. She was afraid to hope, but she leaned to look inside.

A weak lantern lit the tiny space. A woman rested on a blanket while a man hammered a stake in a corner of the tent.

"Mr. Wong?" Lily called.

He turned and looked puzzled when he saw Lily standing in the tent's open flap.

"I'm Lily Chen . . . May's friend." The word sounded strange but felt true after all they'd been through. "We've been looking for you."

Mr. Wong's face lit with hope. "My children are here? They are safe?"

Lily nodded. "But Lee is hurt. He's at the hospital with May. I can take you."

Mr. Wong knelt by his wife and spoke quietly to her in Cantonese. Then he followed Lily and Ranger back through the crowds to the hospital.

When they arrived, May ran to her father and hugged him so fiercely she almost knocked him to the ground.

The news was better now. Another doctor had come and given Lee medicine to keep him from getting sicker. He was propped up in bed, sipping broth.

May told her father the story of their day. Then Mr. Wong asked the nurse, "Can my boy be moved safely? We have family in Oakland. We had hoped to get a ferry today, but when we were separated, I feared that . . ." He pressed

his lips together and shook his head. "My family is together now. That is what matters."

The nurse nodded. "His fever should go down soon, and his leg is splinted. If you can find a cart and horse to take you to the ferry landing, he should be fine."

"Very good news," Mr. Wong said.

Lily nodded. But somehow, the good news was squeezing her heart into a tiny lump. May and Lee would leave the burning city in the morning. They'd take a ferryboat across the sparkling bay to Oakland, where family awaited them. Lily's family was far, far over another ocean. Somehow, she'd find her way back to Lo Mo and the other girls, she supposed. But it wasn't home.

Mr. Wong took a deep breath and let it out in a long, quiet whistle. He looked at May. "The store will be gone when we return," he said. "Chinatown will burn to the ground by morning. All our things . . ." He shook his head, then looked up suddenly. "The papers! You brought them, yes?"

"Oh, Father! Here!" May reached into her bundle of clothes and pulled out the thick envelope she'd brought from the store. "I'd left them behind, but Lily and I ran back to save them."

Mr. Wong stared at the papers. "What a good, brave daughter I have," he said. Then he looked at Lily. "Thank you for helping her. For saving my family's future. And my son."

Lily nodded. But her eyes started to fill with tears, and she had to turn away.

May reached out and squeezed her hand. "Father," she said. "Lily should come with us! When she stopped to help me, she lost her group from the mission house where she lives. They're not her real family, though, and she has no way to find them now. If she comes with us, she can help me care for Little Brother while you and Mother make plans. And then . . ." May looked at Lily. "Perhaps she could join our family and work with me at the store after school, once we rebuild. We'll need more hands while Little Brother heals."

The words swarmed in Lily's head. Come to Oakland . . . Join our family . . . Store . . . *School!* It was too much to hope for. Lily shook her head. "You wouldn't want —"

But Mr. Wong interrupted her. "You helped my children. You must let us help you as well. Would you like to stay with us?"

Lily swallowed hard. The huge lump of hope in her throat wouldn't let her speak. But she nodded.

May flung her arms around her.

Ranger leaned into the girls, and they wrapped him in their hug.

"Oh, Lily!" May said. "Mother always says that some good comes out of every terrible thing. And now we're going to be sisters!"

A siren wailed outside. Someone shouted into the tent, and the doctors went running.

"What is it?" Mr. Wong asked a nurse racing by.

"The wind's changed directions!" she called over her shoulder. "The fire's spreading this way!"

Lily swallowed hard. She held tight to May's hand and tried to think about morning. Mr. Wong would hire a horse and cart. They'd travel through the ruined city, board a ferry, and sail away to Oakland. The fires would go out. They'd rebuild Chinatown. Lily and May would go to school together and work side by side in the new store.

But first, they'd have to survive the night.

Chapter 15

THE FERRY'S FAREWELL

No one slept.

Mr. Wong stayed by Lee's side. Lily, May, and Ranger went back to the canvas tent and huddled with Mrs. Wong in the flickering shadows.

The fires burned all night but never reached the park.

In the morning, the girls found Mr. Wong slumped against Lee's cot, asleep. Lee was awake and looking better. The medicine, the hot broth, and a good night's sleep had given him strength.

Mr. Wong left and returned an hour later with an impatient cart driver and a sturdy-looking brown horse. The horse pawed the dirt, and the man tapped his foot as Red Cross workers loaded Lee into the cart. Mrs. Wong climbed in, too. They loaded bundles of clothes and bedding, the packet of papers May had saved, the tiny gold canary in its cage, a suitcase full of things Mr. Wong had brought from the store, and a satchel of coins he'd carried through the burning streets. Then they set off for the ferry dock.

The cart was full, so Lily, May, and Ranger walked along behind it with Mr. Wong. The wheels stirred up clouds of dust and ash, but Lily barely noticed. She was used to the heavy, gray air.

Traveling through the city was like walking through a nightmare. The earthquake and fires had transformed familiar landscapes into twisted versions of home. The cart lurched so violently over cracks in the street that Lily feared it might be shaken to pieces.

Finally, they rattled and bounced their way to the foot of Market Street. Crowds waited to board the morning ferries. Lily held tight to May's hand as they inched their way toward the boat.

"Come now, it's time to board," Mr. Wong said. He lifted Lee from the cart and into a smaller wagon someone had found to get him to the boat. He helped Mrs. Wong down from the cart and held her arm as they shuffled toward the dock.

Lily climbed up into the cart to get her bundle and the canary. The little bird fluttered over to her side of the cage.

"Hello, little one," Lily whispered, and pushed her finger through the bamboo bars.

The canary poked gently with its beak — a

tiny peck of a kiss. Then it flitted away to another perch. And it sang.

Cheery-hee! Cheery-hee!

Swee! Swee! Chirree!

"May, do you hear?" Lily couldn't take her eyes off the little bird. It was the most hopeful song she'd ever heard.

Whirr-chee! Whirr-chee!

Cheekeo-cheekeo-whooo!

"It's lovely!" May said. "But Father is waiting!"

Lily picked up the cage, hopped down from the cart, and hurried after the Wong family.

"Passengers only!" a crew member shouted as they neared the gate. "There's no space for trunks or bags!"

Mr. Wong left his suitcase in a heap of abandoned belongings. He tucked his sack of coins and the family's papers into his coat. May dropped her bundle of clothes, and Lily did the same. She set down the canary's cage, unlatched the door, and slowly put her hand inside. A few of the bird's delicate golden feathers whispered around the bottom of the cage. Lily picked one up and tucked it into her pocket. Then she held her finger at the edge of the cage. "Come on now . . . come with me."

The little bird sang one last time — *chirree-ree-sweet* — and hopped onto its new perch. Lily cupped her hand around him to protect him from the bumping crowd. Then she turned to Ranger. "Ready for a boat ride, dog?"

Mr. Wong took out coins to pay, but the ferry was free today. The officer waved them through. Lily was last in line. When she started forward, the officer held up his hand.

"Passengers only!" he barked, and pointed down at Ranger.

"But . . ." Lily stopped. "I can't leave him behind."

"Then you'll have to stay. There's no room for dogs!" The officer pushed her aside so other passengers could keep boarding.

Lily dropped to her knees beside Ranger, still cupping the tiny bird in her hands and holding him close to her chest. What was she supposed to do? "I won't leave you," Lily whispered, burying her face in Ranger's neck. "I won't . . ."

Ranger felt Lily shaking with sobs. He felt the little bird twitching between them. He listened to the buzz of the people and the blast of the ferry's horn. Then he heard May's voice.

"Lily! Hurry!" She was waving from the boat. But Lily didn't look up. Ranger shook her gently away from him. Then he licked her hand and looked up at the boat.

Lily looked up, too. She saw May waving and motioning. Ranger nudged Lily toward the boat.

"You're telling me to go on, aren't you?" she whispered. "You've helped us so much. Of course you'll be all right taking care of yourself, too."

Ranger barked and leaned his body against her. Lily needed to go. *Now.*

Lily uncupped her hands — the bird stayed perched on her finger — and wrapped an arm around the shaggy dog's neck. "Be safe, dog. And thank you." She stood, then hesitated, and reached into her pocket. "In China, we have an old proverb that says, 'To walk a thousand li and present a swan feather; the gift is light but the friendship is solid.'"

She tucked the tiny yellow canary feather under Ranger's collar. "I don't have a swan feather for you, so this will have to do for now, my friend. Perhaps you'll find us again one day."

"Lily!" May called again from the boat.

Lily curled her hands around the bird, tucked it under her shirt, and walked through the gate.

Ranger watched her board. He listened as the great ship blasted its horn and pulled away from the dock. The crowd was still buzzing. The soldiers were still shouting. But there was another sound, too.

A quiet hum.

Ranger found the bundle Lily had left behind and nuzzled it open. There with her clothes and a thin wool blanket was his first aid kit. The humming was getting louder and louder.

Ranger nuzzled the strap over his neck, and

the humming buzzed louder still. The old metal box grew warm at Ranger's neck, and light spilled from the cracks.

He looked up at the ferry again.

It was getting smaller already, taking Lily and May across the big bay to a city that wasn't on fire. They were safe now. It was time for Ranger to go home.

The humming grew louder, and the light from the box got brighter and brighter. *So bright!* Ranger had to close his eyes.

When he opened them, Luke was standing in the mudroom with a bundle of old clothes.

Chapter 16

HELPING AT HOME

"You coming with us, Ranger?" Luke tipped his head toward the door. Mom's van was running in the driveway.

Ranger's first aid kit had stopped humming. He lowered his head, dropped it into his dog bed, and trotted outside after Luke. Ranger sat in the far back with the boxes of freshly washed clothes Luke and Sadie were donating. The laundry soap smell made him sneeze. That made Sadie laugh, and that made Ranger very happy to be home.

When they got to the church, people were sorting box after box of clothes and books and toys into baskets for the refugee families. Ranger followed Luke and Sadie up to a table and waited while the volunteers decided who could use their hand-me-downs.

"One of our new families just arrived," a woman told Sadie, and pointed toward a picnic table under the Sunday School oak tree. "Would you like to go say hello?"

Luke and Sadie walked over to the table. There was a boy about Sadie's age and another who looked a little older than Luke. Then there was a younger girl, maybe four or five years old, and a baby asleep in her mother's arms.

"Hi!" Sadie waved as they approached. "I'm Sadie and this is my brother, Luke."

"And this is Ranger," Luke said. "You can pet him if you want. He's friendly."

The children didn't pet Ranger. They looked a little afraid of him, but the mother smiled at Luke and Sadie. Then she said, "English . . ." She held up her fingers close together to show she only understood a tiny pinch of what they'd said. She put a hand on her chest and said, "Yara."

Then she pointed to the younger boy. "Ammar." His older brother was Sayid. The little girl was Sabeen, and her baby sister Amira.

"Luke," said Luke, with a hand on his own chest. He smiled and pointed to Sadie and said her name, too.

Sadie pointed at the swing set on the church lawn. "Want to play?"

The children looked at their mother. She nodded, and they raced across the lawn to the swings. Ranger sat down in the shade to watch. Sabeen hesitated a moment, staring at Ranger.

Her eyes were dark and curious, like Lily's. One of her brothers called to her, and she ran to a swing.

The children slid down the slide and climbed over the monkey bars until Luke and Sadie's dad called them. It was time to go home for supper, so they said good-bye and piled into the van.

"That was fun," Sadie said. "They're nice. I hope they like it here."

"Me too," Mom said. "I'm sure they miss their home terribly. But we'll do all we can to make them feel welcome."

"Maybe they'll like soccer," Luke said, and leaned back to pet Ranger. "Hey . . . you've got a feather stuck in your fur." He pulled the tiny bright canary feather from under Ranger's collar. "You haven't been chasing birds, have you?"

Mom looked over her shoulder. "That

doesn't look like it's from one of the robins or sparrows that visit my feeder," she said, "Maybe it fell off a fancy hat someone donated at the church."

Ranger gave a quiet bark and nuzzled Luke's hand. Luke laughed as they pulled back into their driveway. "Don't worry . . . you can have it back. I know how you are about the stuff you find. I'll even carry it to your dog bed so you don't get it all drooly."

They went inside, and Luke dropped the feather over Ranger's blanket. It drifted back and forth and came to rest in a fold beside the other gifts from children Ranger had met on his journeys. Ranger pawed his blanket over the treasures.

Then something light brown and fluffy caught his eye in the window.

Ranger barked.

"What's up, boy?" Luke said. "You want to go back out and play?"

Ranger did. Because Lily was safe now, in her new home with the Wong family. His work was finally done.

And there was still time to chase a few squirrels before supper.

AUTHOR'S NOTE

Lily Chen and May Wong are fictional characters, but their story is based on dozens of letters and recollections written by people who experienced the great San Francisco earthquake of April 18, 1906. The earthquake itself lasted only fifty seconds, but it broke the city's water lines, so the fires that followed swept through the city for three days before they were finally stopped.

While the earthquake and fires devastated nearly all of San Francisco, the people of Chinatown faced extra hardships because of discriminatory laws in place at the time. The Chinese Exclusion Act of 1882 banned

Photo credit: National Archives and
Records Administration

Photo credit: United States
Geological Survey

most Chinese from coming to America. The
few exceptions included merchants, teachers,
students, and family members of those who
were already in the United States. As a result,

many Chinese boys and girls were sent to the United States with forged papers. Like Lily, these "paper sons" and "paper daughters" sometimes ended up as servants and were treated poorly.

Donaldina Cameron — or Lo Mo, as she was known to the girls and women in her care — was a real Presbyterian missionary who made it her business to rescue Chinese girls and women who were being kept as servants. Once the girls were freed, however, they had to follow strict rules at Cameron's mission house. They were rarely allowed outside, were trained in skills the missionaries thought they'd need to be good wives, and could leave only when they married a suitable Christian man. I imagine that the mission home would have been a difficult place for someone like Lily, who had different dreams. Cameron remains a controversial figure in San Francisco's Chinese American community today. People I spoke with appreciate her dedication but criticize her negative views of Chinese men and the way she imposed Christianity and Western culture on the girls and women in her care. The mission house on Sacramento Street burned in the 1906 fires but was rebuilt in the same

location and operates as a community center in Chinatown today.

May's desire to save her family's papers is also based on real historical accounts. At the time of the earthquake, Chinese people were required to carry certificates proving that they were in America legally. If a person happened to be stopped by immigration officials and didn't have those papers, there was a chance they could be deported or sentenced to hard labor. As a result, some Chinese residents of San Francisco risked everything to go back into dangerous areas to save their papers as the flames spread.

But the fire clouds also had a silver lining for many of San Francisco's Chinese residents. Immigration records and birth certificates were destroyed when City Hall burned. They all had to be reissued, and many Chinese workers who had been barred from becoming Americans took advantage of that. By claiming that they were born in the United States but their birth records had been destroyed in the flames, they were finally able to gain citizenship. That's because the Fourteenth Amendment to the United States Constitution, which was ratified in 1868, stated that any person born in the United States was eligible.

The earliest letters and reports about earthquake refugees describe a mix of cultures all camped out together in the city's parks. But it wasn't long before the city set up a separate camp to segregate Chinese people at the Presidio. For years before the earthquake, city leaders had been talking about moving Chinatown to a less desirable piece of land away from the city's financial district. The city saw the earthquake and fire as a perfect opportunity to make the idea a reality. But residents of Chinatown caught wind of the plot and made plans of their own — to rebuild Chinatown in its original location before the city fathers could act. Under the leadership of a businessman named Look Tin Eli, they got a loan from Hong Kong and designed the new Chinatown in an architectural style that would bring in

tourists. The plan worked, and Chinatown rose from the ashes to become the community it remains today — buzzing with new immigrants and longtime Chinese American residents as well as tourists enjoying festivals, markets, museums, and restaurants.

The Chinese Historical Society of America on Clay Street has a wonderful small museum that explores the stories of the Chinese in America. I'm most thankful to historian and storyteller Charlie Chin, who spent an afternoon with me, sharing details of early-twentieth-century Chinatown and discussing Lily's story.

The California Historical Society's research library has a wealth of 1906

earthquake resources. I spent a glorious two days there, poring over photographs and handwritten letters. Many of the details of Lily's story — trunks being dragged along, a couch being pushed up a hill — come from these primary sources. I was amazed by the stories of people who fled from the fires, carrying their bundles of bedding and wearing their Easter hats.

I think my favorite moment in all those hours of research had to do with the canaries. I'd read at least a dozen letters whose writers mentioned seeing people carrying

birdcages. It puzzled me that this was so common. Did *everybody* in 1906 San Francisco have a pet canary?

Later, I came across a letter that Etoile Millar Blauer wrote to her school friend, Hazel Aubry, on April 20, 1906. Blauer had been visiting relatives in Oakland when she was awakened by "a terrible roaring sound" and shaking that sent a large bust of President McKinley crashing to the floor. She described her aunt's dramatic reaction: "Aunt Jenny, wild-eyed, with her hair streaming down her back and clad only in her nightgown, appeared in the doorway screaming 'God save the children!' and threw herself across the bed."

Etoile Blauer tried to take a ferry back home to San Francisco to find her mother, but officials weren't letting anyone enter the city. Medical personnel were the only ones allowed. Undaunted, Blauer borrowed a white linen dress from her aunt, made a cap out of one of her uncle's starched collars, and boarded the ferry disguised as a nurse. When she arrived in San Francisco, she joined the parade of people in the streets, all trying to flee the fires.

"Since we have become refugees we have seen hundreds of people with canary birds in cages," she wrote in her letter. "A man told us today that Robinson's Pet Shop had just received a large shipment of canary birds, and rather than let them perish in the fire they had given them to the passers-by who would take them."

The mystery of the canaries was solved! I knew that if Lily passed by that pet shop, she would have helped, too. A quick check of a 1906-era city map told me that Robinson's Pet Shop had indeed been located on a street that might be part of Lily and May's journey. I was thankful to be able to include such a moment of hope in a dark and difficult chapter of the story.

Even though the people of San Francisco lost so much in the 1906 earthquake and fires, those moments of hope are present in their stories, too.

Hugh Kwong Liang was a teenager when the Great Earthquake began on that April morning. He left Chinatown for Nob Hill and was then sent to the Presidio. Like Lily, he watched the flames grow closer and feared for his safety. Liang walked to the nearby waterfront, where he spotted a boat, snuck on board, and hid under a table. When he was discovered halfway across the bay, the crew treated him with kindness until the boat arrived in Napa.

"Before I left the boat," Liang recalled, "the men took up a collection of coins and gave it to me with their best wishes. I shall never forget their kindness. I awoke to the fact that those men were the real Americans. They were so nice and considerate. It was a far cry from the race prejudice and harsh discrimination that I knew. Perhaps there is hope that things will get better with me."

FURTHER READING

To read more about the 1906 San Francisco Earthquake and working dogs like Ranger, check out the following books and websites:

I Survived the San Francisco Earthquake, 1906 by Lauren Tarshis (Scholastic, 2012)

If You Lived at the Time of the Great San Francisco Earthquake by Ellen Levine (Scholastic, 1992)

Sniffer Dogs: How Dogs (and Their Noses) Save the World by Nancy Castaldo (Houghton Mifflin Harcourt, 2014)

The Earth Dragon Awakes: The San Francisco Earthquake of 1906 by Laurence Yep (HarperCollins, 2006)

"The 1906 San Francisco Earthquake and Fire" via the National Archives and Records Administration: https://www.archives.gov/exhibits/sf-earthquake-and-fire/

"The Great 1906 San Francisco Earthquake" via the United States Geological Survey: http://earthquake.usgs.gov/regional/nca/1906/18april/index.php

"Timeline of the San Francisco Earthquake" via the Virtual Museum of the City of San Francisco: http://www.sfmuseum.org/hist10/06timeline.html

SOURCES

I'm most grateful to the Chinese American scholars and friends — Beatrice Chen from the Museum of Chinese in America, Charlie Chin from the Chinese Historical Society of America, Wendy Shang, and Vincent Ling — who helped me with Lily's story by answering questions or reviewing the manuscript. The following sources were also incredibly helpful:

Barker, Malcolm E., comp. *Three Fearful Days: San Francisco Memoirs of the 1906 Earthquake and Fire.* San Francisco: Londonborn Publications, 1998.

Bronson, William. *The Earth Shook, The Sky Burned: A Photographic Record of the 1906 San Francisco Earthquake and Fire.* San Francisco: Chronicle Books, 2006.

Choy, Philip P. *San Francisco Chinatown: A Guide to Its History and Architecture.* San Francisco: City Lights Publishers, 2012.

Fradkin, Philip L. *The Great Earthquake and Firestorms of 1906: How San Francisco Nearly Destroyed Itself.* Berkeley: University of California Press, 2005.

Hansen, Gladys and Emmet Condon. *Denial of Disaster: The Untold Story and Photographs of the San Francisco Earthquake and Fire of 1906.* San Francisco: Cameron and Company, 1989.

Jorae, Wendy Rouse. *The Children of Chinatown: Growing Up Chinese American in San Francisco, 1850–1920*. Chapel Hill: The University of North Carolina Press, 2009.

Morris, Charles, ed. *The 1906 San Francisco Earthquake and Fire: As Told by Eyewitnesses*. New York: Dover Publications, 2016.

Schwartz, Richard. *Earthquake Exodus, 1906: Berkeley Responds to the San Francisco Refugees*. Berkeley, CA: RSB Books, 2005.

Tchen, John Kuo Wei. *Genthe's Photographs of Old San Francisco's Chinatown*. New York: Dover Publications, 1984.

Winchester, Simon. *A Crack in the Edge of the World: America and the Great California Earthquake of 1906*. New York: HarperCollins, 2005.

Yung, Judy. *Unbound Feet: A Social History of Chinese Women in San Francisco*. Berkeley: University of California Press, 1995.

About the Author

Kate Messner is the author of *The Seventh Wish*; *All the Answers*; *The Brilliant Fall of Gianna Z.*, recipient of the E. B. White Read Aloud Award for Older Readers; *Capture the Flag*, a Crystal Kite Award winner; *Over and Under the Snow*, a *New York Times* Notable Children's Book; and the Ranger in Time and Marty McGuire chapter book series. A former middle-school English teacher, Kate lives on Lake Champlain with her family and loves reading, walking in the woods, and traveling. Visit her online at www.katemessner.com.

Don't Miss Ranger's Next Adventure:
D-DAY: BATTLE ON THE BEACH

Ranger travels to Normandy on the morning of the D-Day invasion and finds himself in the middle of one of the fiercest battles of World War II. In the midst of the chaos, he meets a Jewish boy who's hiding with a local farmer, and a young American soldier fighting to free France from the Nazis. Turn the page for a sneak peek!

planes away. Walt and the other men had practiced launching and maneuvering the car-sized balloons. The plan was to raise them over the beaches of Normandy, where the balloons would form a sort of defensive curtain in the sky, protecting Allied troops from German planes.

And now it was time.

The night journey across the sea had been dark and murky, but suddenly, the sky lit up in the distance. Searchlights swept the cliffs. The air thundered with the pounding of bombs.